# Watch out for Witches!

*Also by Hilda Offen in Happy Cat Books*

The Trouble with Owls

# Watch out for Witches!

## Hilda Offen

HAPPY CAT BOOKS

*Published by*
Happy Cat Books
An imprint of Catnip Publishing Ltd.
Islington Business Centre
3-5 Islington High Street
London N1 9LQ

This edition published 2006
1 3 5 7 9 10 8 6 4 2

A CIP catalogue record for
the British Library
ISBN 10: 1 905117 17 5
ISBN 13: 978-1-905117-17-8

Printed in Poland

# Contents

*For Angela Morse*

# The Fairy Godmother's Advice

The King of Little Twittelburg threw open the window.

"A new prince is born!" he cried. "Send for the Fairy Godmother!"

All day long invitations sped to the four corners of the kingdom. Carrier pigeons thronged the air. The telephone lines buzzed. Bells rang out. And all day long a steady stream of well-wishers flowed into the palace.

"Where's she got to?" grumbled the King, looking at his watch.

Towards evening a loud fanfare of trumpets sounded, and in strode a tall woman with a briefcase. She wore a smart business suit and there was a green orchid in her button-hole.

"Better late than never!" muttered the King. Aloud he said, "Welcome, welcome, dear Fairy Godmother!"

"Never mind all that!" she snapped. "Time's money. Where's my fee?"

The King handed her an envelope. "I think you'll find it's all there," he said.

"It had better be!" said the Fairy Godmother. "Now – where's the baby?"

"Over here," said the King, waving at the royal cradle. "Er – what are you going to wish him?"

"Oh – the usual!" said the Fairy Godmother. She unsnapped her brief-case. "Good Looks, Good Manners and Common Sense. What's his name?"

"Florian Dorian," said the King.

"Peregrine Pom –" added the Queen. She was going to say "Pomroy" but the Fairy Godmother cut her short.

"Florian Dorian Peregrine Pom!" she cried, waving her wand. "I wish you Good Looks –"

But now it was her turn to be interrupted. The curtains billowed in a sudden draught and the candles began to flicker. Blinding lights flashed in the air and a terrible smell filled the room. There was a scratching and a rumbling – and then a voice boomed out from the floor. It was as loud and as sudden as a foghorn and it made everybody jump.

"We'll make you sorry!" hissed another, softer voice.

"Your child is doomed!" cried a third.

"Wait till he's eight years old!" yelled a fourth. "He'll go into the wood!"

The smell got stronger and stronger.

"And he won't come out!" cried a fifth voice. Scratch! Scratch! Scratch! "He'll be ours for ever and ever!"

There was a horrid cackling sound and the curtains billowed once more. Then a silence filled the room; all that was left was the smell.

"Witches!" said the Fairy Godmother. She was already fastening her briefcase.

Pandemonium broke out. People rushed backwards and forwards. The baby started to howl.

"Help us!" cried the King, clutching the Fairy Godmother's arm. "Aren't you meant to know about this sort of thing?"

"What do you expect me to do?" asked the Fairy Godmother.

"Lift the spell!" said the King.

"Sorry!" said the Fairy Godmother. She looked at her watch. "I have to be at the next palace in twenty minutes."

The King threw himself at her feet.

"Please!" he cried. "Please, please, please!"

"Get up!" snapped the Fairy Godmother. "Don't grovel. The spell cannot be changed – what is done is done."

Prince Florian Dorian Peregrine Pom howled louder than ever.

"None the less," said the Fairy Godmother, "I can give you some advice – for a small fee, of course."

The King handed her a five-pound note.

"Well – what is it?" he cried.

Everyone waited with baited breath. Even the young prince stopped crying.

"Never let Prince Florian go into the wood," said the Fairy Godmother and she hurried off to a waiting taxi. "And watch out for witches," she called as her taxi sped away.

"What a cheek!" said the King. "That was a complete waste of money!"

"Anyone could have told us that!" said the Queen. "That's common sense!"

You may have noticed that the Fairy Godmother had forgotten to finish her three wishes. We'll hear more about that later.

While all this was happening, a baby girl was born to an ordinary family called Jones. They lived in an ordinary house in an ordinary street just beneath the palace walls.

"What shall we call her?" asked Mr Jones, peeping at his new daughter, who was sleeping peacefully in her cot.

The King spent a sleepless night. When morning came he sat up in bed.

"I know – we'll cut down the wood!" he cried.

"What a good idea, my dear!" said the Queen.

The King sent for an army of woodcutters and gave them their orders. Off they marched, through the town and into the wood beyond. In no time at all they were back again.

"It's no good," said the foreman. "It can't be done. The trees are like iron – our axes just bounce off them."

"A fence!" cried the King. "That's what we need – a fence all around the wood!"

But that was no good either. No sooner had the workmen set the posts in the ground than invisible hands wrenched them up and threw them away.

"Our son must never go into the wood," said the King.

"We must tell him," said the Queen. "Over and over again until he gets the message."

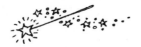

The young prince started to grow. No one called him Florian any more – they called him "Pompom" instead. It seemed to suit him better.

"Don't go into the wood!" said his nurse as the prince sat on his potty.

"Don't go into the wood!" said the cook, as she served the prince his boiled egg.

Prince Pompom made a rude face and threw his buttered "soldiers" on the floor.

He was a beautiful child. He had big blue eyes and a cloud of golden hair. But he had no manners. And he had no common sense.

"Don't go into the wood!" wrote his tutor on the blackboard.

Prince Pompom stuck out his tongue and scribbled all over his worksheet.

"Don't go into the wood!" whispered his parents as they kissed him goodnight.

But Prince Pompom put his fingers in his ears. "Da-dee-da-dee-da-da!" he chanted. "I can't hear you!"

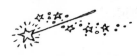

# The Itchy Witch

The years passed quickly. On Prince Pompom's eighth birthday the King and Queen threw a huge party. There were balloons and streamers and a red banner that ran the length of the hall. A message was written on it in gold letters. It said "Don't go into the wood."

The band struck up and the singer launched into a song specially written for the occasion.

If you stray away from the palace
You're sure to come to no good,
So whatever you do, don't roam
   from home
AND DON'T GO INTO THE
   WOOD.

Prince Pompom sat eating jelly with an ugly scowl on his face.

"I *shall* go if I like!" he thought. "I bet

there's something really nice in there they don't want me to find – treasure or sweets or something!"

"Now we're all going to play Hide and Seek!" called the Queen.

The grown-ups put their hands over their eyes and started counting up to twenty. The children ran and hid. Some got under tables, some got behind curtains and others got into cupboards.

Prince Pompom did none of these things. He ran out of the banqueting hall, out of the palace and over the moat. No one saw him go. He ran through the town and straight into the wood.

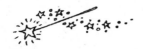

After a while the prince stopped running and looked about him. Primroses bloomed amongst the tree-roots and birds were nesting in the branches overhead.

"Bo*ring*!" said Prince Pompom.

He left the path and plunged deeper into the wood.

"Stop!"

The prince looked up in surprise. Before him stood a witch. She was dressed all in black, except for a curling green feather that sprouted from her hat. She had a ferocious scowl on her face and she was scratching and wriggling like mad.

Prince Pompom gave her a haughty stare.

"Cheeky little whippersnapper!" snarled the witch and she grabbed Prince Pompom by the scruff of the neck and dragged him onto her broomstick.

Then she flew away to a glittering tower, all covered in fish-scales, that stood beside a river.

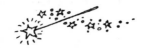

The witch threw Prince Pompom into a mean little room at the top of the tower. It had only one tiny window and a solid oak door.

"Let me go!" cried Prince Pompom.

"Here you are and here you stay!" said the witch, wriggling around and scratching.

"I won't! I won't!" shouted Prince Pompom. He glanced out of the window.

"I shall grow my hair!" he said. "A princess will climb up it and rescue me!"

The witch gave a grim laugh.

"You've been reading too many Fairy Tales, sonny," she said.

She took a pair of scissors from a shelf.

"Just to make sure, though," she said, "I shall give you a weekly haircut. Come here!"

"Help!" cried Prince Pompom, and fainted clean away.

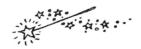

The prince came round to find himself lying on the floor surrounded by locks of golden hair. He touched his head; it felt light and stubbly.

He jumped up and rushed around the little room, kicking at the walls and door and hurting his toes. But it was no use. There was no way out – he was trapped.

Every day the witch visited him. She brought with her a packet of cheese sandwiches and a plastic bottle filled with mineral water.

"Don't want anything!" said the prince sulkily.

"Please yourself! I'll leave it here anyway," said the watch, and off she went, locking the door behind her.

The weeks passed. Time dragged. Prince Pompom was really, *really* bored. He never wanted to see another cheese sandwich in his life.

Then one day he noticed something in his tunic pocket. He took it out and looked at it. It was the present he had won at "Pass the Parcel" on the day of his party! He tore off the wrappings. Inside was a little writing set emblazoned with the royal crest.

Prince Pompom sat and stared at it for several hours. Then he had an idea. He ripped a leaf from the writing pad and wrote

He took an empty bottle from the pile in the corner and put the message inside. Then he corked the bottle and threw it out of the window. "Plop!" The bottle landed in the water below and was carried away by the current.

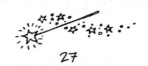

The bottle bobbed away downstream. It travelled through the wood, under bridges and through the town until it came to rest in some reeds. And there it was found by Laura Jones. She was now a big girl of eight and she was hunting for sticklebacks. Laura uncorked the bottle and read the message.

"It must be from Prince Pompom," she thought, noticing the royal crest.

"I'd heard he was missing. I'd better go and rescue him."

She set off upstream. She walked on and on until she came to the glittering tower.

"Ahoy there!" she called. "I've come to rescue you!"

A head appeared at the window.

"It's the prince!" thought Laura. "And he's got a punk haircut!"

"Go away!" cried Prince Pompom. "I was expecting an army – or a princess. I don't want to be rescued by an ordinary girl like you."

"Well, I'm all there is," said Laura. "And you're lucky to have me – I could hardly read your note. You spell 'desperate' d-e-s-p-e-r-a-t-e, by the way."

"Oh yeah?" said Prince Pompom. ("Who cares?" he thought.)

"I'm coming up!" said Laura.

"You can't!" said Prince Pompom. "The witch has cut off my hair – so you've nothing to climb."

"I'll come up the ordinary way," said Laura. She marched up the winding staircase. The witch had left the key in the lock so she had no trouble opening the door.

"Come on!" said Laura to Prince Pompom. "We've no time to waste."

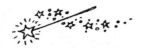

Even as Laura spoke they heard a sound on the staircase.

Scratch! Scratch! Scratch! It was the witch!

"She'll turn us both into toads!" whimpered Prince Pompom.

"No she won't!" said Laura Jones. She pointed at the bottles – some full, some half-full and some empty. "Help me roll these down the stairs!"

Thump! Thud! Bumpity-bump! The bottles bounced from stair to stair, going faster and faster as they went.

The witch lost her footing and rolled all the way to the foot of the stairs.

"You should be ashamed of yourself!" said Laura.

The witch was lying under a pile of bottles. All they could see was the twitchy green feather in her hat.

"Why did you kidnap the prince?" asked Laura, lifting off some of the bottles.

The witch struggled to her feet. She was still scratching.

"Because I'm so angry!" she said.

"And why are you angry?" asked Laura.

"Because of the itch," said the witch. "I can't stop scratching."

"But why do you itch?" asked Laura. "Are you ill? Is it an allergy?"

"It's my underwear!" said the witch. "You'd itch if you had to wear knickers like mine."

She lifted her skirt and Laura saw that she was wearing old-fashioned knickers that reached to the knee. They seemed to be made of some coarse, spiky material.

"Woven from nettles," said the witch proudly. "All the best witches wear them. My vest's the same."

33

"Well, I can help you," said Laura. "But you must promise never to kidnap the prince again."

"It's a deal!" said the witch.

"Then fly us to the High Street," said Laura Jones.

They all sat on the broomstick, one behind the other, and away they flew to town. They left the broomstick at a parking meter and Laura led the way into a shop that went by the name of "Smartypants".

"*My* knickers are made of cotton," said Laura to the witch, "and I never get itches."

"Cotton! How common!" muttered Prince Pompom. "My boxer shorts are made of silk."

The sales lady came bustling out with her tape-measure and measured the witch. She placed a selection of underwear on the counter and the witch chose some white cotton knickers and a vest to match. Then she went into the changing room. After a while they heard her laughing and then the curtain swished back.

"I've changed!" she cried.

"You certainly have!" said Laura.

The witch had stopped wriggling; there was a broad grin on her face.

"They're so comfortable!" she cried, giving Laura a hug. "I feel wonderful! It's the first time in three hundred years I haven't had to scratch!"

The witch selected a further six sets of underwear, in pink, blue, yellow, green, lilac and navy.

"That will be fifteen pounds," said the sales lady.

The witch took three newts from

her pocket and placed them on the counter.

"Aargh!" cried the sales lady. "What are they?"

"Bank-newts, of course," said the witch; and even as she spoke the newts stopped being newts and turned into three five-pound notes instead.

The witch skipped out of the shop with her purchases under her arm; then she hopped on her broomstick and did a vertical take-off.

"Goodbye!" she cried. "And thank you!"

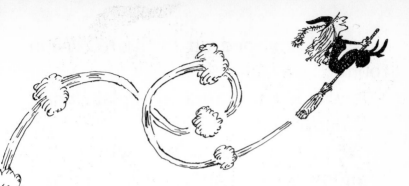

She looped the loop and flew away over the roof-tops. They stood listening to the sound of her laughter as it faded away into the distance.

"So that's that sorted out!" said Laura to Prince Pompom.

Laura escorted the prince back to the palace. The King and Queen came rushing out to meet them.

"Oh – your beautiful hair!" wailed the Queen. "What happened to it?"

Prince Pompom ignored his anxious parents.

"I'm going to watch Blue Peter," he

said and stomped off to the television room.

It was left to Laura to explain what had happened.

"You seem like a girl with some common sense, Laura Jones," said the King. "Here's a gold sovereign for you."

Laura curtseyed.

"And good manners, too," said the Queen.

"Our son has neither sense nor manners," said the King. "Do you know what the children hereabouts say when they want to insult each other?"

"No, Your Majesty," said Laura. (She did really, but she thought it best not to mention it.)

"They call each other 'A right Pompom'," said the King. "They do! I've heard them!"

"It's all the fault of that Fairy Godmother," said the Queen.

"I'm terribly afraid," said the King, "that Prince Pompom will try and go into the wood again. Would you keep an eye on him for us?"

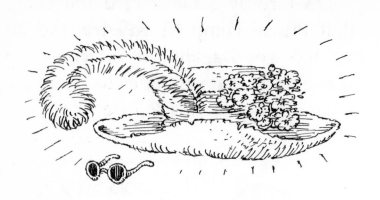

# The Multi-Coloured Witch

The King was quite right. Prince Pompom just couldn't keep his nose out of trouble. He waited until his tutor had gone to get some chalk from the stock-cupboard and then he was off again. Of course, he headed straight for the wood. He hadn't gone far when he noticed he was being followed by Laura Jones.

"Go away!" cried Prince Pompom. "I do not wish to be followed by an ordinary girl like you!"

He wasn't at all grateful to Laura for rescuing him the day before.

"As you like, Your Highness," said Laura. "I'll just collect a few things for the school nature table – then I'll be on my way."

The prince walked off with his nose in the air. After a while he came to a woodland pool. He sat down and stared at his reflection in the water; he fancied his hair was beginning to grow again.

"I really am very nice-looking!" he thought.

Suddenly the surface of the pool began to flash with colours. Reflected in the water Prince Pompom saw another witch! She was standing right behind him.

This one was quite different from the last. She was dressed in all the colours of the rainbow and more besides; and to make it worse, all the colours clashed. She wore a purple jumper with orange spots and a green skirt with red and silver stars all over it. There was a pink ostrich feather in her yellow hat and her boots were gold, with blue and purple laces.

But it didn't end there! Her hair was pink, with green and mauve streaks, and her fingernails shone with bright turquoise varnish. As for her face – ugh! Her nose was painted purple, her cheeks green, and she wore fluorescent blue lipstick. She was an *awful* sight!

Prince Pompom, who wore only the most tasteful colours (he was dressed by his valet) put his hands over his eyes. That was when the witch pounced. She grabbed the prince and dragged him towards a multi-coloured car.

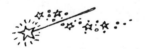

Laura Jones had been watching all this from the bushes. She took some sun-glasses from her satchel and popped them on. They shielded her eyes nicely from the glare.

The witch was already starting up the car.

"Aha! She's left the boot open!" whispered Laura, and she tip-toed forward and climbed in.

Vroom! Vroom! The witch revved up the engine and then they were off, swerving wildly round oak trees and frightening rabbits.

At last the car screeched to a halt outside a multi-coloured castle.

"Come with me!" said the witch and she dragged Prince Pompom out of the car and up a dazzling flight of stairs.

Laura climbed out of the boot and followed at a safe distance, dodging behind pillars and statues.

The witch flung open a multi-coloured door.

"Good heavens!" gasped Laura.

Prince Pompom and the witch were standing on the threshold of a vast ballroom – and there inside were a hundred princesses and ninety-nine princes, dancing as though their lives depended upon it. Round and round they danced, moving to some unseen music that played in the air above their heads.

"Meet my hundredth prince!" said the witch; and as the youngest princess danced past she grabbed her and pushed her and Prince Pompom together.

As soon as their hands touched they were glued fast. They were swept up into the dance – round and round they whirled, going faster and faster.

Prince Pompom was a terrible dancer.

"Stop treading on my toes!" snapped the youngest princess.

"You're treading on mine!" said Prince Pompom. ("This is a nightmare!" he thought. "I'm going to wake up in a minute.")

"Dance!" cried the witch. "Dance! Dance, my lovelies! Dance forever!"

She climbed the stairs to a gallery above the ballroom. There she sat, as though bewitched herself, studying the swirling dancers below.

Laura Jones had been watching all this. Now she crept up the stairs and addressed the Multi-Coloured Witch.

"Excuse me!" she said. "Just what do you think you're doing?"

The witch gave a little cry and jumped to her feet.

"You're trespassing!" she said and she let loose a dozen multi-coloured spells. The air around them crackled with lights – purple, blue, green and pink – but Laura didn't budge. She kept her sun-glasses on and frowned at the witch, her arms folded.

"Why have you kidnapped all those princes and princesses?" she asked.

"I haven't kidnapped them," said the witch. "I just collect them, that's all."

She aimed some pink and yellow fireballs at Laura, but they bounced off and dissolved into thin air.

"You must know it's wrong to keep them here," said Laura.

Suddenly the witch buried her head in her hands and began to cry.

"No one wants to be friends with me," she sobbed. "I know why it is – I haven't got any colour sense. No one can bear to look at me."

"I'm looking," said Laura Jones.

"But you're wearing dark glasses," said the witch, sobbing louder than ever.

Laura handed her a tissue and the witch blew her nose. When she had recovered a little she said:

"I can't help collecting them! They're so beautiful."

She pointed down at the ballroom.

"Look at the way they're dressed. I keep looking and looking and I keep hoping that one day I'll get the hang of it, but nothing seems to happen."

Laura looked down. The whirling clothes beneath her had been designed by all the best fashion houses. The princes and princesses wore soft, flowing fabrics in the most delicate colours imaginable – pastel blues and misty mauves, faintest rose and silver, gentle browns and greys.

"You're right!" said Laura. "They *are* beautiful!"

The witch sniffed.

"I think your trouble," continued Laura, "is that you're trying too hard. Would you like me to help you?"

"Oh – if only you would!" cried the witch, clasping her hands.

"If I do," said Laura, "you must promise to set all the princes and princesses free."

"I promise!" said the witch. "Cross my heart and hope to die!"

"Then I think I'd better have a look at your wardrobe!" said Laura Jones.

The witch whisked Laura up to her bedroom in a multi-coloured lift.

"Oh, Witch! Really!" said Laura, looking around.

There were clothes everywhere. They spilled out of cupboards and wardrobes, onto the floor, over chairs and across the bed. And the colours! There were reds and blues, oranges and purples, pinks, greens and yellows; there were flower prints and animal prints and gold and silver fabrics; there were spots and checks and zig-zags – there were stripes and sequins and tartans.

"I've never seen anything like it," said

Laura. "Never mind, let's sort your face out first."

She sat the witch down at her dressing-table and she creamed away all the ghastly colours – the fluorescent blue lipstick, the purple nose and the green cheeks.

"We'll just add a touch of lip gloss," she said. "There – that's all you need. Now – if you go and wash the colours out of your hair I'll find a dress for you."

Laura hunted around amongst the piles of clothes until she found a simple blue dress with a flowing skirt. She laid it out on the bed along with some colour charts she found in her satchel. The humming of a hairdryer came from the bathroom. After a while the witch appeared. Her hair was now a soft golden brown.

"Oh – that's much better!" said Laura. "Would you like to try on this dress?"

The witch slipped the blue dress over her head and pirouetted round and round.

"Why, Witch – you're beautiful!" said Laura.

The witch caught sight of herself in a full-length mirror and stopped twirling.

"I can't believe it's me!" she gasped.

They went downstairs to the ballroom. The witch snapped her fingers – Once! Twice! Thrice! – and the spell was broken. The music faded away and the dancers came gliding to a halt. When they saw the new-look witch, all the princes (with the exception of Prince Pompom, of course) fell at her feet and begged her to marry them.

"Thank you, but no," said the witch. "I am going to study these colour charts Laura Jones has given me. Then I am

going to redecorate the whole castle. I shall be much too busy to get married."

She threw open the doors and the princes and princesses streamed away through the wood.

"I can't wait to get started," said the witch. "But first, I'll drive you home."

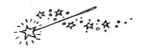

"Oh, Pompom!" said the King as Laura walked in with their son. "You're back!"

"Thank goodness you're safe!" cried the Queen.

Prince Pompom pushed them away.

"I'm going to play Sonic Ferret," he said. "Send the Royal Physician to the video room – my feet are killing me."

The King took Laura to one side and insisted she told him the whole story.

"You've done well, Laura Jones," he said when she had finished. "Have another sovereign. But please continue to watch our son. I fear he may do something silly."

"I think you may well be right, Your Majesty," said Laura Jones.

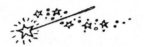

# The Smelly Witch

"The time has come," said the King, "to start dropping heavy hints."

"The time has come," said Prince Pompom, "for a snack."

But when he went to the fridge, there, pinned to the door by a banana-shaped magnet, was a note. It said "Don't go into the wood."

At bedtime his old nurse took to reading him stories like *Little Red Riding Hood* and *Goldilocks and the Three Bears*.

"You see, Your Highness," she said, "it really isn't safe to go into woods."

"The forecast for today is thunderstorms," announced the voice of Radio Twittelburg in the morning. "Trees will be struck by lightning. So don't go into the wood."

There were notes beside Prince Pompom's plate, inside his shoes, and under his pillow. There were even notes in the lavatory; he found them hidden in the toilet roll.

Prince Pompom was extremely annoyed by all of this. He waited until he thought no one was looking and then off he went to the wood.

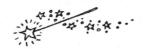

Laura Jones's Auntie Ray had phoned that morning and asked Laura to visit her.

"I've got a late birthday present for you," she said.

They were standing in the garden under the clothes line.

"There's a terrible smell coming from the wood today," said Auntie Ray. "I shall have to ring the council – hello! Isn't that Prince Pompom?"

"Yes, it is!" said Laura. "Thanks for the present, Auntie Ray – I'll have to go. Can I borrow a clothes peg?"

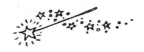

The smell was getting stronger and stronger.

"Phew!" said Prince Pompom. "I can't stand this any more. I'm going home."

He turned round – and there stood Laura Jones. She was wearing a clothes peg on her nose.

"You're following me again!" screamed the prince. "And what are you doing with that clothes peg? You look ridiculous!"

"Id's the sbell," said Laura, talking through her nose. "Id's awful, isn'd id?"

"Leave me alone!" shouted the prince, and he ran away into the undergrowth.

Laura followed him, taking care to keep well out of sight.

The smell grew stronger still. It was accompanied by a strange rattling sound.

Suddenly a witch appeared. She was riding a bicycle with a basket on the front and she wore an old blue boiler suit and wellington boots. On her head was a bowler hat with a fish bone stuck in the brim. Her hair was long and greasy and there seemed to be bits of eggshell tangled up in it.

When she saw Prince Pompom the witch leaped from her bike.

"Well met, my pretty!" she cried and flung her arms around him.

The smell was so awful that poor

Prince Pompom fainted right away. The witch popped him into her bicycle basket and rode off amongst the trees.

Laura ran along behind. It wasn't difficult keeping track of the witch – all she had to do was take the clothes peg off her nose and follow the smell.

The witch stopped outside a cave and carried Prince Pompom inside. She dropped him into a chair carved from a solid lump of gorgonzola cheese.

"Here you are and here you stay!" she cried.

"I won't!" shrieked Prince Pompom, who had recovered from his faint. "You smell! Pooh! It's horrible!"

"You rude creature!" cried the witch. She hopped around in a temper.

"Just you wait! I'll turn you into a cow pat! Or a pair of sweaty socks! Or a rotten old kipper!"

"Nod so fasd!"

The witch whirled round. Laura Jones stepped from behind a stalagmite. She had put the clothes peg back on her nose.

"My name's Laura Jones!" she said. "Look here, Widch, you can'd durn the prince indo a piece of smelly old fish!"

"I can if I like!" yelled the witch. "And then I'll stick him under the grill! And then I'll feed him to the cat! He insulted me! He said I smelled!"

"I don'd want do sound rude," said Laura. "Bud you are a bid pongy."

"Now *you're* doing it!" yelled the witch. "I'll turn you into a stink bomb!"

She waved her hand and aimed a host of smelly spells at Laura. But Laura stood with her arms folded and the clothes peg on her nose.

The witch whirled round and round like a spinning top. Terrible fumes filled the air. Then she toppled over and fell across the table.

"No one visits me!" she moaned. "I'm so lonely!"

"I'm not surprised!" said Prince Pompom. "I don't suppose anyone can bear to come near you."

"Please be quied, Your Highness," said Laura. "You're in enough drouble already. Please leave this do me."

Laura removed the clothes peg from her nose.

"Can I ask you something personal?" she asked.

"What is it?" sniffed the witch.

"How often do you wash your hair?" asked Laura.

"Once a week!" said the witch. "I

use a special shampoo I make myself from eggs. It's meant to give your hair a lovely shine – I read all about it in a magazine."

"Hmm!" said Laura. "What sort of eggs do you use?"

"Oh – all sorts!" said the witch. "Any old eggs I can find. I spend hours riding about collecting them in my basket. Look!"

She flung open a cupboard door. It was full of eggs – hens' eggs, wrens' eggs, sparrows' eggs and owls' eggs. A lot of them were cracked. A horrible smell drifted out.

"Aha!" said Laura. "Now we're getting somewhere!" She said gently, "I think you're meant to use fresh eggs."

The witch looked astounded.

"And I've another question for you," said Laura. "How often do you bath? And what do you bath in?"

"I bath regularly," said the witch. "Once a week. And I bath in a bath, of course."

"I mean, what do you use in your bath?" said Laura. "Soap, bubble bath, bath salts—"

"Oh, nothing like that," said the witch. "I make my own herbal baths. They're very good for you. I read about them in the magazine."

"How do you make them?" asked Laura.

"I'll show you," said the witch eagerly. "Come with me!"

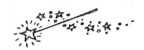

The witch led the way to an inner cave. There was a bath in one corner; it was filled to the brim with a bright green bubbling liquid. Green vapour drifted from the surface and hung in the air. Words alone cannot describe the smell – it was *awful*.

"You bath in that?" gasped Prince Pompom, looking over Laura's shoulder. The witch ignored him.

"It's very good," she said to Laura. "I spend the week collecting odds and ends to put in it – deadly nightshade, hemlock, viper's bugloss, old cabbage leaves – you know the sort of thing. I was going to drop the prince in, too – I thought he'd add a certain something."

"Oh!" said Prince Pompom and fainted away again.

"Though now I've seen him," said the witch, "I'm not so sure."

"Help me carry him back to the table," said Laura. They placed the prince in a chair and Laura made the witch sit down too.

"This bathing business," said Laura. "I don't think you're going about it the right way."

"No?" said the witch.

"No," said Laura. "But I've got something here you might find useful."

She reached into her satchel and brought out Auntie Ray's present. It was prettily wrapped in silver paper and tied with a blue bow.

"What is it?" asked the witch.

"Unwrap it and see," said Laura. "Auntie Ray gives me the same present every year."

The witch tore off the paper. Inside was a bar of pink soap, a pink flannel, a bottle of shampoo and some bubble bath.

"I'd like you to try them!" said Laura.

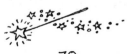

Laura emptied the bath tub and scrubbed it out. Then she ran a fresh bath. She tipped in the bubble bath and handed the witch the soap and flannel.

"Try the shampoo on your hair while you're in there!" she said. "I think you'll find it easier to use than the eggs!"

The witch stepped into the bath tub.

"Er – I think you should take your clothes off first," said Laura. "And your boots."

"Really?" said the witch, amazed. "I never have before."

"There's a first time for everything," said Laura.

The witch undressed and hopped into the bath.

"Oooh! It's lovely!" she cried. "I didn't know baths were meant to be nice! I've never really looked forward to them. I shall do this at least three times a day in future!"

"Can I ask you something else,

Witch?" asked Laura. She was holding the witch's boiler suit between her finger and thumb.

"Ask away!" burbled the witch, up to her chin in bubbles. She peered at Laura through the steam.

"How often do you change your boiler suit?" asked Laura. "And your boots?"

"Oh – never!" said the witch. "I keep them on all the time – even in bed. They're my favourite clothes."

"That's another mistake, I'm afraid," said Laura. She went into the other room and started to rummage around in a wardrobe.

"There's a whole pile of new boiler suits here!" she called. "All in different colours, too."

"Yes, there's one for every day of the week," said the witch. "But I'm afraid I never got past Monday."

"Well, I think you should try Tuesday, at least," said Laura. "And try putting your boots out to air at night."

"All right!" said the witch, who was shampooing her hair. She started to sing *I'm Forever Blowing Bubbles*.

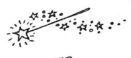

Laura found some slippers and a fluffy bath towel in the wardrobe. She put them to warm in front of the fire, along with a yellow boiler suit. Prince Pompom had recovered from his faint, so she got him to help her load the eggs into the witch's bicycle basket. They wheeled them down the garden and emptied them onto the compost heap.

"How are you getting on?" called Laura, back in the cave once more. She carried in the warm things and left them beside the bath. Then she and the prince toasted crumpets on the fire. After a while the bathroom door opened and out came the witch in a cloud of steam. A towel was wrapped around her head and she wore the yellow boiler suit and slippers. She looked rosy and clean, and she smelled – oh! the smell!

"Mm! You smell just like a bunch of spring flowers!" said Laura.

"Is that a good smell?" asked the witch uncertainly.

"Well – it's better than the last one!" said Prince Pompom.

"It's lovely!" said Laura.

Then they sat round the fire and ate the crumpets.

The witch took them back to the palace on her bicycle. Laura sat in the basket and Prince Pompom sat on the crossbar. He complained all the way.

The King and Queen were pacing anxiously about the banqueting hall. Prince Pompom rushed past them crying, "Ugh! You've no idea what I've had to put up with today! Cook! Bring me a hamburger!"

"You've done very well, Laura," said the King when he had heard her story. "Here's your gold sovereign. But keep your eyes open. Something tells me the danger is not yet past."

And he was quite right . . .

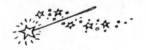

# The Noisy Witch

"Laura Jones is a very reliable girl," said the King to the Queen. "But we can't expect her to watch our son every minute of the day. We must make sure that Pompom is never left on his own."

Prince Pompom soon found that his every move was watched. Wherever he went, up popped a footman, or a cook, or a man-at-arms, saying "Not that way, Your Highness." He just couldn't escape from the palace.

He decided to get up at the crack of dawn one morning and give everyone the slip.

He awoke to the sound of his alarm clock (he had hidden it under the pillow) and crept out of his room and down the hushed corridors. As he tip-toed through the hall the cuckoo-clock struck four.

"Cuckoo! Cuckoo!" it creaked.

Prince Pompom noticed that the cuckoo was holding a sign in its beak. It said

*Cuckoo!*

*Cuckoo!*

DON'T GO INTO THE WOOD

"All's well! All's well! On a fine midsummer morning!" bawled the night-watchman as the prince sped through the deserted streets. "But don't go into the wood!"

Now, just by chance, the watchman's cries woke Laura Jones. She glanced out of the window and spotted the prince scurrying past.

"Uh-huh!" said Laura to herself and, pausing only to pull on some clothes and to pop a few things into her satchel, she set off after the prince.

The wood looked lovely. Thousands of fresh spiders' webs sparkled in the dew.

"Horrid things!" said Prince Pompom and he slashed at them with a stick. He hated spiders. Indeed, he hated them so much that the King had been forced to appoint a Royal Spider Catcher.

"Your Highness! Stop it!" called Laura Jones.

Prince Pompom whirled round in a rage.

"Spiders don't do any harm!" said Laura.

"I hate them," said Prince Pompom. "And I hate you. Why do you keep following me?"

"I'm collecting mini-beasts for my school project," said Laura. She held up a jam jar filled with cotton-wool.

"Mini-beasts!" said Prince Pompom. "You're a mini-beast! Stop bothering me!" And he ran away as fast as his legs would carry him. At last, out of breath, he stopped to slash at another web.

"STOP!" roared a voice. It was the loudest voice Prince Pompom had ever heard. It was like a foghorn. He looked around; there wasn't a soul in sight.

"STOP!" roared the voice again.

It seemed to be coming out of the ground. Prince Pompom looked down.

There at his feet stood the tiniest witch he had ever seen. She was not much taller than the average mouse.

"STAY WHERE YOU ARE!" roared the witch in her enormous voice. "I'M GOING TO PUT A SPELL ON YOU!"

She danced round and round, waving her wand. Prince Pompom felt a tingling sensation through the thin silk of his stockings.

"Oh yeah?" he said, rubbing his ankles. "You and whose army? I'm not afraid of you, Titch – I'm going home."

He turned on his heel and stopped, rooted to the spot with horror. There, dangling a few inches in front of his nose, was the biggest, hairiest spider he had ever seen!

"Get him, Malcolm!" said the witch.

Prince Pompom found he could not move a muscle; he was paralysed with fright.

"You know what to do, Malcolm," said the witch, and the spider set to work.

It ran round and round the prince, spinning out its web. In no time at all Prince Pompom was trussed up in a giant cocoon. All you could see of him was his face and the tips of his toes. The witch hopped onto a tree stump.

"Now!" she said. "I'm going to sing to you!"

She took a deep breath, opened her mouth and sang.

"TWINKLE, TWINKLE, LITTLE STAR!" bawled the witch.

She went on and on. It was awful. Prince Pompom was in agony – he couldn't even put his fingers in his ears.

Now – where was Laura Jones while all this was happening? Well, she had heard the sound of the witch's voice – you couldn't miss it. It carried the length and breadth of the kingdom. Over trees and rocks and houses it travelled, over hills and valleys. It bounced off the distant mountains and came booming back again.

Laura stole forwards and peeped out from behind a fallen log. The sound was almost unbearable. She took some cotton-wool from her jam jar and stuffed it in her ears.

"That's better!" she thought. She could still hear the witch's voice; but now it sounded faint and muffled. She jumped over the log.

"Stop!" she cried. "What are you doing?"

The witch fell off the tree stump in surprise.

"HOW DARE YOU INTERRUPT MY

PERFORMANCE!" she cried, scrambling to her feet. "I'LL PUT A SPELL ON YOU!"

She danced around, waving her wand, but Laura was wearing sensible thick socks and the spells couldn't get through.

"That's enough!" said Laura.

She bent down and picked the witch up – very gently – between her forefinger and thumb and popped her into the jam jar. Then she dropped Malcolm in too, and screwed the lid down tight.

She took the cotton-wool out of her ears.

"Let me out!" screamed the witch. Her voice sounded faint and far away.

"What about me?" cried Prince Pompom, hopping around in his cocoon.

Laura opened her satchel and took out a pair of scissors. "Snip! Snap!" In no time at all she had cut through the cocoon and Prince Pompom struggled out. He was puffing and blowing and looked very red in the face.

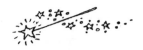

Laura placed the jam jar on the tree-stump and she and the prince peered into it. Prince Pompom shuddered.

"That Malcolm's an ugly creature!" he said.

"No he's not!" said Laura. "He's beautiful. Have a look through my magnifying glass."

"No thanks!" said Prince Pompom.

"Let us out!" yelled the witch. "We'll suffocate!"

"No you won't," said Laura. "There are holes in the lid. And there's cotton-wool for you to sit on, so you'll be quite comfortable. Why were you torturing Prince Pompom?"

"Torturing?" cried the witch. "*Torturing*? It was meant to be a treat."

"You could have fooled me," said Prince Pompom.

"I love singing," said the witch, "but I can never get anyone to stop and listen to me."

"I'm not surprised," said Prince Pompom. "You've got a horrible voice."

The witch's lower lip began to quiver. Malcolm looked worried and stroked her shoulder.

"There, there," said Laura. "But you can't just go around tying people up and singing to them, you know."

"It's the only way I can get an audience," said the witch. "Besides, I was sure that in time the prince would have learned to love my voice. He would have begged me to go on and on."

"Ugh!" said Prince Pompom. "You cannot be serious!"

"I don't want to offend you," said Laura to the witch, "but your voice is very loud."

"But I'm so small!" said the witch. "I have to shout to get people's attention. Squirrels are always running off with me – I have to make myself heard."

"I'm much bigger than you," said Laura, "but I don't sing anything like as loud. Listen to this."

And she sang *Twinkle, Twinkle, Little Star* all the way through.

The witch applauded. "That was very nice," she said.

"If you like the sound of a sick brontosaurus wailing," muttered Prince

Pompom, who couldn't sing at all.

"I wish I could sing like you," said the witch.

"I'm sure you could," said Laura, "with a little practice. If I help you, do you promise to stop tying people up and singing to them?"

"I promise!" said the witch.

Laura unscrewed the jar and tilted it. The witch and the spider slid out and landed on the tree stump. Prince Pompom ran and hid behind an oak.

"If you're really serious about learning to sing," said Laura, "you should start by practising your scales."

"*Scales*?" said the witch. "What are they?"

Do-ray-me-fa-so-la-te-do!

"Oh – that sounds beautiful!" said the witch, clapping her hands. "Could you teach me to do that?"

"I should think so," said Laura. "In fact, I have a little rhyme that helps me remember my scales. Would you like me to teach it to you?"

"OH, YES PLEASE!" bawled the witch, overcome with excitement.

"Sh!" said Laura. "Listen to this, then." And she started to sing.

"'Dough' is what you use for bread
'Ray' – that stands for Auntie Ray.
'Me' is someone I know well,
'Far' is miles and miles away.
'Sow' is what you do with seeds,
'La's a word that I don't know,
'Tea's what follows after lunch
And now we've fallen in the dough!"

Prince Pompom skulked behind the oak with his fingers in his ears. He watched Laura and the witch as they danced in and out of the trees, singing Laura's rhyme. Malcolm danced after them. Every time they got to the last line they fell down, waved their legs in the air and screamed with laughter.

"Yuk!" said Prince Pompom and closed his eyes tight.

After a while Laura said to the witch,

"I think you've got it."

"HOORAY!" boomed the witch.

"But you still need more practice," said Laura. "My teacher, Miss Crotchet, taught me to sing. I'm sure she'd give you a few lessons."

"Then please take me to her!" said the witch.

So Laura put the witch on one shoulder and Malcolm on the other and set off for town. Prince Pompom trudged after them with a face like thunder.

When they reached Miss Crotchet's house, Laura rang the bell and called through the letter-box.

"Miss Crotchet! Do you mind spiders?"

"Love 'em!" said Miss Crotchet, opening the door. "Now, what have we here?"

"A new pupil!" said Laura.

Malcolm had already swung down to

the doormat on a gossamer thread and the witch was sliding down after him.

"Wonderful!" said Miss Crotchet. She bent over the witch. "Do you know your scales, my dear?"

DO-RAY-ME-FA-SO-LA-TE-DO!

"Lovely! Lovely!" said Miss Crotchet. "Still a little bit of work to do – let's make a start, shall we?"

She ushered the witch into the house. Laura lingered for a while on the doorstep.

"Do introduce me to your friend," she heard Miss Crotchet say. "I've never seen such a magnificent-looking mini-beast in all my life!"

"I think they'll get on very well," said Laura to Prince Pompom as they made their way back to the palace.

Prince Pompom did not reply.

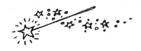

The King and Queen were having breakfast. They hadn't even realised their son was missing.

"Pompom, our dearest boy!" they cried. "Where have you been?"

But Prince Pompom pushed them aside and rushed off to have a row with the Royal Spider Catcher.

"OK! OK!" they heard him yelling. "So you've fixed all the spiders in the palace! Now I want you to start on the wood."

"I don't know what we'd do without you, Laura," said the King. "Take this sovereign – you've certainly earned it."

The Queen sighed.

"If only the Fairy Godmother had finished her wishes," she said. "Perhaps we could get her back."

The King put his arm around her shoulders.

"It's hopeless, my dear," he said. "No one has seen her for the last eight years. It's as though she just disappeared into thin air."

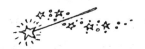

# The Greedy Witch

"You will stay in your room all day!"
said the King to his son. "It's for your
own good."

Prince Pompom threw a tantrum.
He kicked his valet and rolled on the
floor, but the King would not budge.
He locked Prince Pompom's door with
a golden key. The prince's yells could
be heard throughout the palace.

That evening there was a beautiful sunset; the skies to the west blazed with fire. Laura Jones stood at her window and watched the swans flying home to the Royal Lake.

Suddenly her eye was caught by a slight movement to her left.

"Hello – what's that?" she wondered, and she trained her binoculars on the palace walls.

A tiny figure was sliding down a rope of knotted sheets.

"It's Prince Pompom!" said Laura. She watched as the prince dropped into a dinghy and rowed across the moat. "He's off again!"

She took her torch and set out for the wood.

Laura soon caught up with Prince Pompom. He was idling along, kicking at glow-worms.

"You again?" snarled the prince. "What are you doing here?"

"Studying moths," said Laura. "They're part of my school project. Look."

She shone her torch and instantly a thousand fluttering wings started to circle in its beam.

"*Boring!*" said Prince Pompom. He was eating a large bag of bulls-eyes. He made no move to offer one to Laura. He just stood there, scowling.

"I don't know why my parents think you're the bee's knees," he said. "You're a real drag. Leave me alone, will you?"

Even as he spoke there was a rush of wings. A giant owl swooped out of the darkness and snatched up the prince in its talons. Then it flapped away amongst the trees.

Help! Help!

screamed Prince Pompom. His cries faded slowly into the night.

"Oh dear!" said Laura. "How will I find him this time?"

Then she noticed something stripey gleaming in the darkness. She shone her torch at it. It was a bulls-eye!

"There must be a hole in the bag," thought Laura.

A bit further on she spotted another sweet, then another . . . and another . . .

She set off to follow the trail through the wood.

The owl flew on through the night with Prince Pompom dangling from its talons. After a while the prince noticed a neon sign flashing amongst the trees. He half expected it to say "Don't go into the wood", but it didn't. It said "Greedy-Guts Cafe". The sign was fixed over the door of a rickety shack.

The owl swooped down and landed

on the roof and as it did so, someone came to the door.

"What have you brought for me tonight, Wesley?" she called.

In answer, the owl let go of Prince Pompom. He slithered down the roof and landed with a "Thud!" at the feet of the fifth witch.

She was enormous. She wore a leather-studded jacket over a check overall, and on her head was a base-ball cap with "Greedy-Guts" written across the front. She was rubbing her hands together and chortling with delight.

"You've done well, Wesley!" she said. "This time next week we'll have Pompomburgers on the menu! That'll bring in the customers!"

Prince Pompom was still stunned from his fall. The witch tucked him under her arm and carried him inside the cafe.

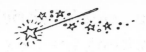

Prince Pompom came round to find himself inside a wooden cage. The witch had just locked the door and was pocketing the key. The table on which the cage rested was covered with all sorts of cooking equipment – knives, rolling pins, frying-pans and pudding bowls.

"Oink!"

Prince Pompom twisted round. To his horror, he found he was sharing his cage with a small pig.

"Let me out!" shrieked Prince Pompom, rattling the bars of the cage.

"Certainly not!" said the witch.

She had started to paint a huge sign which said: "All this week – Pompomburgers and Porkyburgers! Only the best at the Greedy-Guts Cafe".

She washed out her paintbrush and stuck it behind her ear.

"All I have to do now," she said, "is fatten you up. Eat this cream bun!"

"No I won't!" screamed Prince Pompom and he threw it back at her.

"Very well, the pig can have it," said the witch, tossing it back into the cage.

It was while all this was happening that Laura arrived at the cafe. She tiptoed through the overgrown garden and peeped round the door. She saw the prince sitting in the cage, glaring at the pig, and she saw the witch kneading away at some dough.

Laura pushed the door and the bell tinkled as she went in. She sat down at a table.

"Hurray, a customer at last!" said the witch and she whipped out a notepad and a pencil.

"What would you like?" she asked.

"I'll have some baked beans on toast," said Laura.

"Baked beans are off," said the witch. She was reaching into her pocket as she spoke and eating jam tarts.

"Then I'll have scrambled eggs," said Laura.

"Scrambled eggs are off," said the witch.

"Jam tarts are off," said the witch, shoving the last one into her mouth. She wiped her hands on her overall. "If you'd care to wait a week there'll be some lovely Pompomburgers on the menu."

"A week is too long to wait!" said Laura. "This is no way to run a cafe – the tables are greasy! The knives are dirty! And you can't cook the prince!"

"That's right!" called Prince Pompom.

"Can't I just?!" snarled the witch. "Come here – I'll cook you too! I'll turn you into a Bossyburger!"

She made a grab for Laura. Laura jumped up and ran round the table and the witch ran after her. They dodged this way and that, knocking over chairs and trays and pudding-bowls – then

suddenly Laura leaped at the open window and dived through.

"Don't leave me here!" wailed Prince Pompom.

The witch was in such a rage that she didn't stop to think. She dived straight after Laura. What a mistake! The window was really small and she was really big. She stuck fast, half in and half out.

Laura strolled back through the door and took the key from the witch's pocket. She opened the cage and out bounded Prince Pompom, closely followed by the pig.

The witch was struggling and kicking her legs.

"Get me out!" she screamed.

"Only if you promise to stop cooking people," said Laura.

"I promise!" gasped the witch. "I'll never, ever do it again!"

So Laura grasped the witch's legs and pulled. But the witch was so tightly jammed that nothing happened.

"Come on – help me pull, Your Highness!" said Laura.

"She deserves to stay there," grumbled Prince Pompom; but all the same he put his arms around Laura's waist and pulled. Still nothing happened.

Then the pig trotted forward, grasped Prince Pompom's tunic in its mouth and tugged – and out shot the witch, like a cork from a bottle. They all landed in a heap on the floor.

POP!

"Thanks!" said the witch, breathing heavily.

She was silent for a while, then she buried her head in her overall and cried, "That's it, then! I'm finished! I'll never get any customers! No one comes here as it is!"

"I'm not surprised," said Prince Pompom. "Look at the state of the place. I wouldn't be seen dead in here!"

Then he fell silent.

Laura looked around.

"You could turn this into a really nice

restaurant," she said. "What do you usually have on the menu?"

"Oh – anything Wesley catches," said the witch. "Rats, bats, badgers – you know the sort of thing."

"*Rat*burgers!" cried Prince Pompom. "*Badger*burgers? No wonder you don't have any customers!"

"I thought the prince would bring them in," said the witch to Laura. "A touch of class – that's always popular."

"I think you're wrong," said Laura. "I don't think people would like eating Pompomburgers at all."

"Perhaps you're right," said the witch, eyeing the prince. "He doesn't look very nice, does he?"

Prince Pompom made a rude face.

"But what *shall* I feed my customers on?" asked the witch. "I do have other things, like jam tarts, but I get so bored I eat them all myself."

"Well, what about growing some vegetables?" suggested Laura. "You've got a big garden."

"I've never done any gardening," said the witch doubtfully. "Isn't it frightfully hard work?"

"Oh *no!*" said Laura. "My Dad says it's really relaxing. And think of all that fresh air – I'm sure it would do you the world of good."

"Mm," said the witch. "I suppose I might like it. I could give it a go. And I've still got the pig, of course."

"It would be a shame to cook him," said Laura. "He's so sweet. And he did help to rescue you. Why don't you train him to search for truffles instead? You'd make a fortune."

"Brilliant!" cried the witch. "I'll try it!"

"Then let's make a start on the cafe," said Laura Jones.

It was amazing the difference a little elbow grease and some hot soapy water made. Even Prince Pompom joined in and swept the floor, although he did it with a scowl on his face. They scrubbed the tables, found fresh table cloths and washed the knives and forks. At last they stopped to have a cup of tea. They sat back and admired their handiwork. The cafe gleamed like a new pin.

"It looks really great," said Laura.

She and the prince said goodbye and set off through the wood.

They left the witch sitting at a table with her paintbox, designing some new menus.

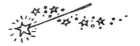

"Laura Jones, you have surpassed yourself!" cried the Queen.

It was long past midnight. She and the King were in their dressing-gowns.

They had noticed their son was missing when they went to kiss him goodnight and they had been waiting up for him ever since.

"Have another gold sovereign!" said the King.

"Thank you, Your Majesty," said Laura.

"Yuk!" said Prince Pompom. "I'm going to bed. Cook! Wake up and bring me some cocoa."

"We're off on our summer holidays tomorrow," said the King. "That should keep Pompom out of trouble for a while. And you can have a rest, Laura."

"Come to tea when we get back," said the Queen.

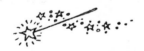

# The Return of the Fairy Godmother

It was a long, lazy summer in Little Twittelburg that year. Laura Jones's parents took her to the seaside.

The Royal Family had gone abroad. Prince Pompom had insisted on a trip to Disneyland.

So it wasn't until the beginning of September that the royal ensign fluttered once more from the palace roof. The

King and Queen had not forgotten their invitation and they sent the Royal Cadillac to collect Laura Jones.

The cook had prepared tea in the banqueting hall. There were cheese straws and fish fingers and baked beans. There was jelly and blancmange. And in the middle of the table stood a giant ice-cream swan with a curving neck.

"Thanks again for all you've done, Laura," said the King, passing her a scone.

"Creep!" muttered Prince Pompom. He was wearing a Mickey Mouse mask. He flicked a spoonful of ice-cream across the table, but Laura ducked and it hit a footman.

At that moment there was a sudden gust of wind and the curtains billowed, just as they'd done on the day of Prince Pompom's birth; but this time there was a difference. Beautiful shifting colours

lit the walls and the scent of spring flowers filled the room. Pleasant laughs rang out and then a sweet voice started to sing *Twinkle, Twinkle, Little Star.*

Laura leaned forward in her chair.

"I know who it is!" she said.

Even as she spoke there was a shower of silver dust – and there before them stood the five witches!

They curtseyed to the King and Queen, and then the first witch spoke.

"Your Majesties!" she said. "Laura Jones is an extraordinary girl! She's changed our lives. Take me, for instance!"

She waved her hand and a trail of silver stars floated through the air.

"I no longer itch – I'm a happy witch!" she said. "I've turned my tower into a helter skelter and the surrounding area is now a fun-fair. Please visit whenever you like – it's all free!"

The second witch stepped forward. She wore a smart lilac suit and a little hat with a veil.

"I am now a dress designer," she said. "People flock to my castle for free fittings. Your Majesties – I have taken the liberty of designing you some new leisure wear."

She laid three track-suits on the table. They were simple and well-cut, and made from soft, amber velvet.

Then the third witch spoke. She was no longer smelly and she glowed from her latest bath. The scent of flowers wafted around her as she moved.

"I have set up a small business," she said, "making bath products and perfumes from wild flowers. I give them away to passing strangers. Please accept a free sample."

She laid a beautifully gift-wrapped parcel on the table.

Then it was the turn of the fourth witch. She spoke in a pleasant voice – it carried well but it was soft and sweet.

"I was Mrs Crotchet's star pupil!" she said. "I went on to join the Town Choir and now I'm their lead soprano. Allow me to sing for you."

Laura lifted her onto the table and the witch stood on a sponge cake and sang *The Teddy-Bears' Picnic*. It was lovely and everybody clapped – everybody except Prince Pompom, that is; he just sat there scowling behind his mask.

Then the fifth witch stepped forward. How she had changed! She was as thin as a rake.

"It's all the digging!" she said, smiling at Laura Jones. "Such good exercise! My vegetarian restaurant is a great success – people drive for miles to eat there! And I'm famous for my truffles! Please do me the honour of dining at 'Magic Munches' next week, Your Majesties!"

"We'd be delighted!" said the King. "I love truffles."

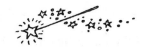

The fourth witch jumped back onto the sponge cake and she sang another song:

> Your Majesties, Ladies and Gentlemen,
> We're giving up magic for good!
> Prince Pompom can go wherever he likes –
> It's safe to go into the wood!

"Who cares?" muttered the prince into his mask. "I'm finished with the boring old wood, anyhow!"

"And it's a great big Thank You to Laura Jones!" cried the first witch. "We've learned a lot from you, Laura."

"And I've learned a lot, too," said Laura. "I've learned about sticklebacks and spiders and moths and owls. I got an 'A' for my project."

The King fell silent and began to look sad.

"All you ladies have learned something from your adventures," he said. "And you, too, Laura Jones. But as for you, Pompom my son, I fear you have learned nothing – nothing at all."

"You learned how to spell 'desperate', didn't you, Your Highness?" said Laura helpfully.

"Yes – d-e-s-p-r-i-t," said Prince Pompom.

The King buried his head in his hands.

As he did so there came the sound of a taxi screeching to a halt outside.

Seconds later the doors burst open – and in marched the Fairy Godmother! "Good Heavens!" cried the King.

"I've been abroad," said the Fairy Godmother. "I've gone international. I was in Transylvania – I'm really big over there, you know – when I happened to pick up the *Transylvania Times*. And there was an advertisement."

"What did it say?" cried the King.

"It said 'FG – return to Little Twittelburg immediately. Unfinished business'," said the Fairy Godmother. "So here I am."

"Who can have placed the advertisement?" asked the King.

Laura stepped forward. "It was me, Your Majesty," she said. "I've been very pleased to keep an eye on Prince Pompom for you, but I was beginning to get a bit bored. I want to have fun! I want to play games! So I advertised in every newspaper I could find."

"But how could you afford it, Laura dear?" asked the Queen.

"I used my five gold sovereigns!" said Laura. "I think it was money well spent."

The Fairy Godmother unsnapped her briefcase. "I checked my records," she said, "and I realised immediately that I'd left something out."

She produced her wand.

"Where's the baby?" she asked.

"Here!" said the King, pushing Prince Pompom towards her.

"My goodness, he's grown!" said the Fairy Godmother.

Prince Pompom tried to dive under the table but the Queen grabbed him.

"We'll get rid of this to start with," said the Fairy Godmother, removing the Mickey Mouse mask and tossing it over her shoulder.

She waved her wand.

"Florian Dorian Peregrine Pom!" she said. "I wish you Good Manners and Common Sense!"

Everyone cheered and clapped. Prince Pompom looked dazed.

"I must love you and leave you," said the Fairy Godmother. "I have to be in Finland by six."

She snapped her briefcase shut.

Then an amazing thing happened. Prince Pompom got to his feet. He went up to the Fairy Godmother and gave a courtly bow.

"Thank you, dear Godmother," he said, "for all the trouble you have taken."

The King and Queen gasped in amazement.

"That's all right, sonny," said the Fairy Godmother, patting him on the shoulder. Then she bustled out of the room.

Prince Pompom turned to the witches.

"And thank you," he said. "Thank you, dear ladies, for everything. I hope to visit you all soon."

The witches curtseyed and then they too took their leave. This time they walked out over the drawbridge like ordinary mortals, leaving a faint scent of primroses and violets in their wake.

The prince bowed before his mother and father.

"My dearest parents," he said. "I fear I have been a sore trial to you. I shall try to do better in future."

"There, there, Florian my boy," said the King, overcome with emotion. Somehow "Pompom" didn't seem to suit his son anymore.

Last of all the prince turned to Laura.

"You've been a real friend to me, Laura Jones," he said. "Can you forget the past?"

"It's forgotten already," said Laura, and they shook hands.

"I'm going to the schoolroom now," said Prince Florian, "to practise my spelling. Then will you come out to play?"

"Great idea, Your Highness," said Laura Jones. "Let's go and try out the witch's helter-skelter!"